MOONSTRUCK

The True Story of the Cow Who Jumped Over the Moon

Gennifer Choldenko

Illustrated by Paul Yalowitz

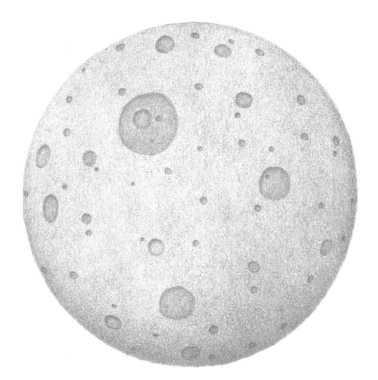

Hyperion Paperbacks for Children
New York

First Hyperion Paperback Edition 1999

1 3 5 7 9 10 8 6 4 2

Printed in Hong Kong by South China Printing Company (1988) Ltd.
The artwork for each picture is prepared using colored pencil.

This book is set in 16-point ITC Usherwood.

Library of Congress Cataloging-in-Publication Data
Choldenko, Gennifer,
Moonstruck: The true story of the cow who jumped over the moon, by Gennifer Choldenko;
illustrated by Paul Yalowitz.
—1st ed.
p.   cm.
Summary: The horse seriously doubts the cow will ever be able
to jump over the moon but offers respect and admiration when the
determined bovine accomplishes that feat.
ISBN: 0-7868-0158-1 (trade)—ISBN: 0-7868-2130-2 (lib. bdg.)-ISBN: 0-7868-1394-6 (pbk.)
[1. Horses—Fiction. 2. Cows—Fiction. 3. Moon—Fiction.]
I. Yalowitz, Paul, ill. II. Title.
PZ7.C446265Mo   1996
[E]-dc20   95-14846

To my dad, James Alexander Johnson
—G. C.

For Dad, Mom, and Sara Lou, too
—P. Y.

Mother Goose . . . what a bag of feathers she is. She makes it sound so easy. Nine hundred forty-one pounds of cow meat, not counting the udder, catapults 240,000 miles to jump over the moon—and what does that old goose woman write? One lousy line—not even a whole poem. I know for a fact the cow was hurt by it, but who am I to say? I'm just an old brown horse. Only *then* I was a young brown horse.

Anyway, I'm getting ahead of myself. I want to tell you the whole story.

First of all, you may not know this, but we horses jump over the moon on a regular basis. Every night at least one of us makes the trip. I don't want to make it sound easy or anything, but we all do it. We can handle it. We're built for it. We begin training from a very early age.

Which is just what we were doing when this cow started hanging around. At first she kept her distance. And, to be quite honest, we were kind of flattered. Who doesn't like an audience?

Then she started trying to get friendly. Asking dumb questions like, "Do you take a running start?" I mean, come on. Whoever heard of jumping clear over the moon from a dead standstill?

Every day she was there, cold weather or warm. As if that weren't bad enough, she began using our equipment herself. That's when I knew I had to have a talk with that cow. I mean, let's face it. Not everyone can be born a horse.

"Look, kid," I said to the cow, "you can't keep doing this. You're going to get hurt. Why don't you go chew the cud with your cow friends?"

"No," she said. "I'm going to jump the moon."

"Honey, come on! You're a cow. Take a look at that body of yours . . . those short little legs, that galumphing stride . . ."

"I don't care," she said. "I'm going to. Every night I look up and say to myself, One day I'm going to see what the moon looks like up close. One day I'm going to jump clear over that moon."

Now I understood. This cow was MOON-STRUCK! There was no use trying to talk sense to her.

"Okay, kid," I said, "I'll give you a shot. But if you can't keep up, you're out. Is that a deal?"

"It's a deal," she said.

I didn't mention this to the others. What—
I'm going to tell them I recruited a *cow* for
the team? I figured she wouldn't last longer
than a day or two anyway. Then we'd be rid
of her for good.

Boy, was I wrong.

First thing in the morning, there she was.
Last thing at night . . . still there.

Every time I'd get ready to tell her to head back to her herd, she'd go and do something really well and I'd have to keep my mouth shut for another day. After a few months, she was jumping as well as the quarter horses. Then what could I say?

So that's how it went for most of the season until we got down to the final part of the training: the Wall.

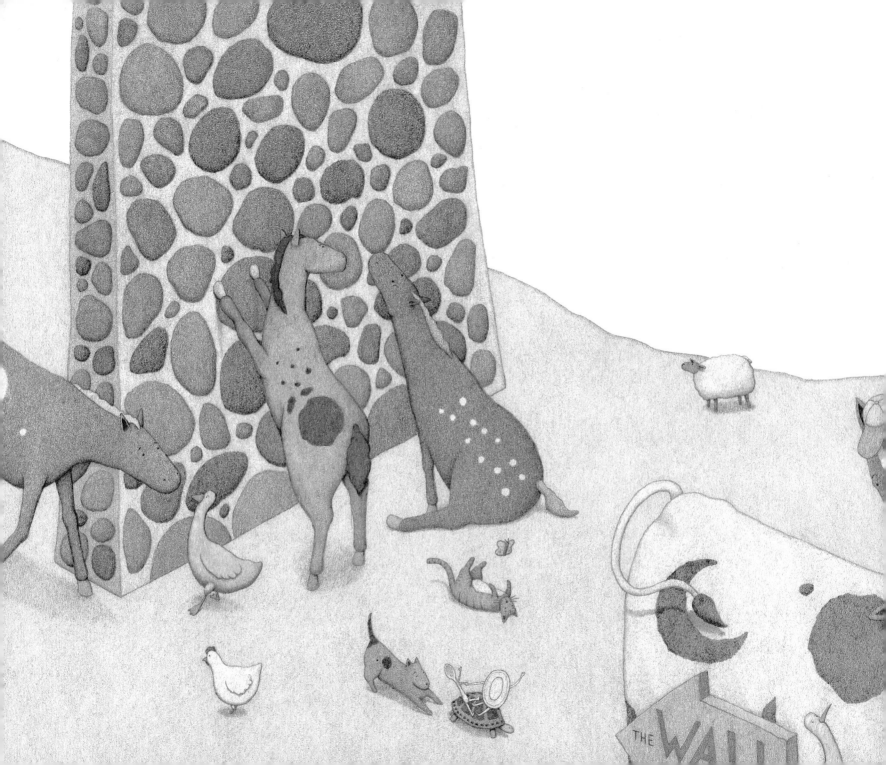

Some of the horses sweat the nails right out of their shoes when it's their turn to jump the Wall. There was no way a cow could clear it, no matter how hard she tried. But when I told the cow that, she galloped off, all in a huff—and I didn't see her again until I was setting up flags for the Wall.

Then all of a sudden there she was, thundering toward the Wall, her cowbell clanking wildly.

"No!" I hollered as the cow gathered her legs under her and sprang all the way over the great stone hurdle.

"Yes! Yes!" the horses shouted, stamping their hooves in salute to that black-and-white babe.

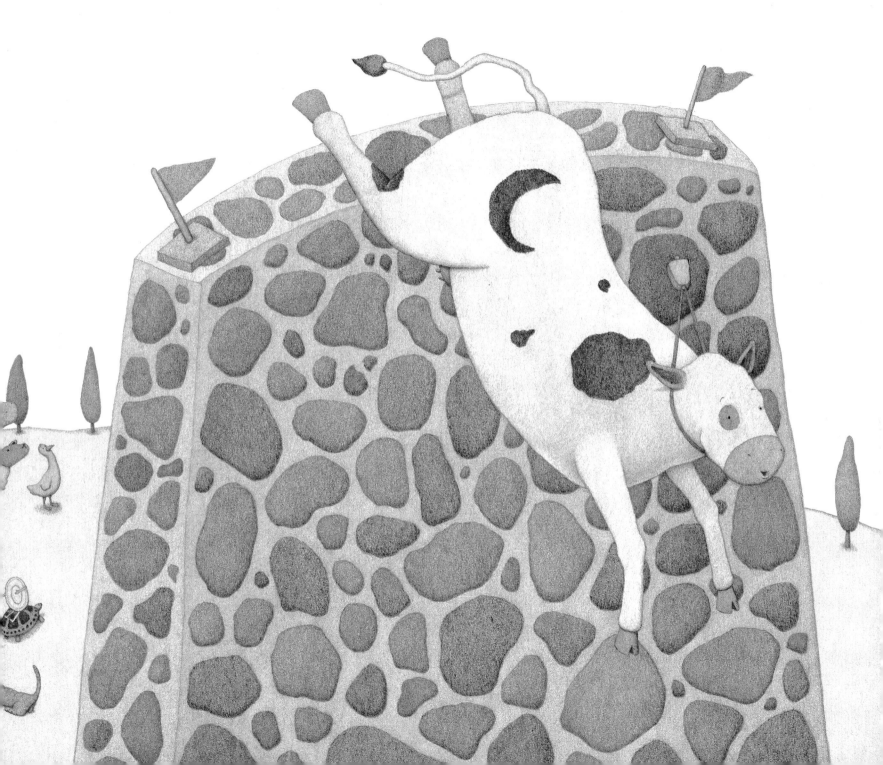

MOON JUMPERS

Victor E.

Sandy Shoes
Rocking Horse
Loco Motive
Hay Basket
Sarah Lou
Trotting Travis
Steven Swift
Miss Cow

After that, I have to tell you, I had to rethink the whole cow thing. Some years half my horses can't clear the Wall and here this crazy bovine jumped it first time out. So that very day I posted a list of the horses who were ready to jump the moon. And on the list I included the cow.

When the cow found out she'd been chosen, you could hear her mooing from one end of the farm to the other. She was so excited, she could hardly keep her mind on schooling those last few days.

But when the night came for her to jump, she was calm and confident, her mind focused on flight.

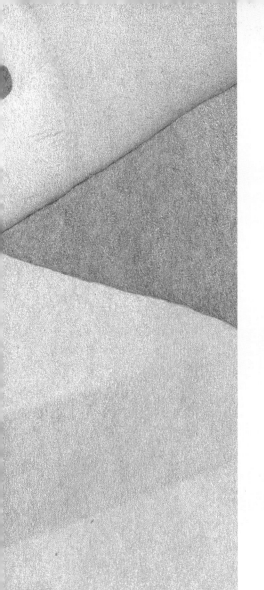

10, 9, 8, 7, 6, 5, 4, 3, 2, 1 . . . **BLAST OFF !**
and she burst forward down the hill.

Faster and faster the cow galloped down the hill. Faster and faster she went as she gathered her legs under her and rocketed into the night.

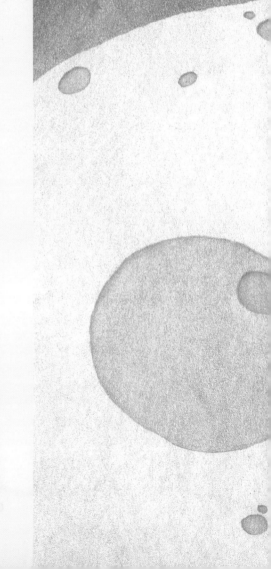

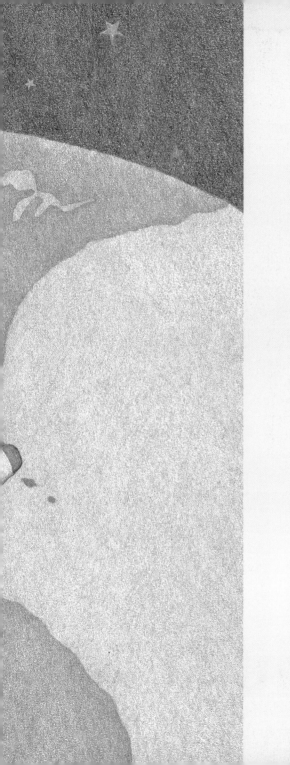

   Higher and higher the cow flew, careening through space at an incredible speed.

   Up and up and up until one, two, three, all four of her stubby legs soared past that big old moon. And then around and around and up and over until she'd seen every bit of the moon up close. And the stars and meteorites and the Milky Way and the Earth . . . And then when there was nothing left to see, gently, gently, gravity brought her back to Earth again.

Well, I can tell you that when she came back, there wasn't a dry eye on the whole planet. Which is why I know for certain that old Mother Goose wasn't around. Because if she'd seen that holstein jump the moon with her own eyes, she wouldn't be wasting her time writing about cats and fiddles and the courtship of dishes and spoons. She would have written a whole book about that cow.